Dear Reader:
I hope you like the book, and even if you don't — Keep READING, keep DREAMING, and keep BELIEVING — in the world, and in yourself! Have Fun ☺
— Dan

To Freddy and George,
who are always full of surprises! —L. R. L.

To my mother, Carmelinda, who remembers what it was like
getting THIS little elephant out of bed. —M. R.

STERLING CHILDREN'S BOOKS
New York

An Imprint of Sterling Publishing Co., Inc.
1166 Avenue of the Americas
New York, NY 10036

Text © 2017 by Linda Ravin Lodding
Illustrations © 2017 by Michael Robertson

ISBN 978-1-4549-1999-5

Distributed in Canada by Sterling Publishing Co., Inc.
c/o Canadian Manda Group, 664 Annette Street
Toronto, Ontario, Canada M6S 2C8
Distributed in the United Kingdom by GMC Distribution Services
Castle Place, 166 High Street, Lewes, East Sussex, England BN7 1XU
Distributed in Australia by NewSouth Books
45 Beach Street, Coogee, NSW 2034, Australia

For information about custom editions, special sales, and premium and corporate purchases,
please contact Sterling Special Sales at 800-805-5489 or specialsales@sterlingpublishing.com.

Manufactured in China

Lot #:
2 4 6 8 10 9 7 5 3 1
06/17

sterlingpublishing.com

The artwork for this book was created digitally and traditionally.

Design by Irene Vandervoort

WAKEY, WAKEY, ELEPHANT!

BY Linda Ravin Lodding

ILLUSTRATED BY Michael Robertson

STERLING CHILDREN'S BOOKS
New York

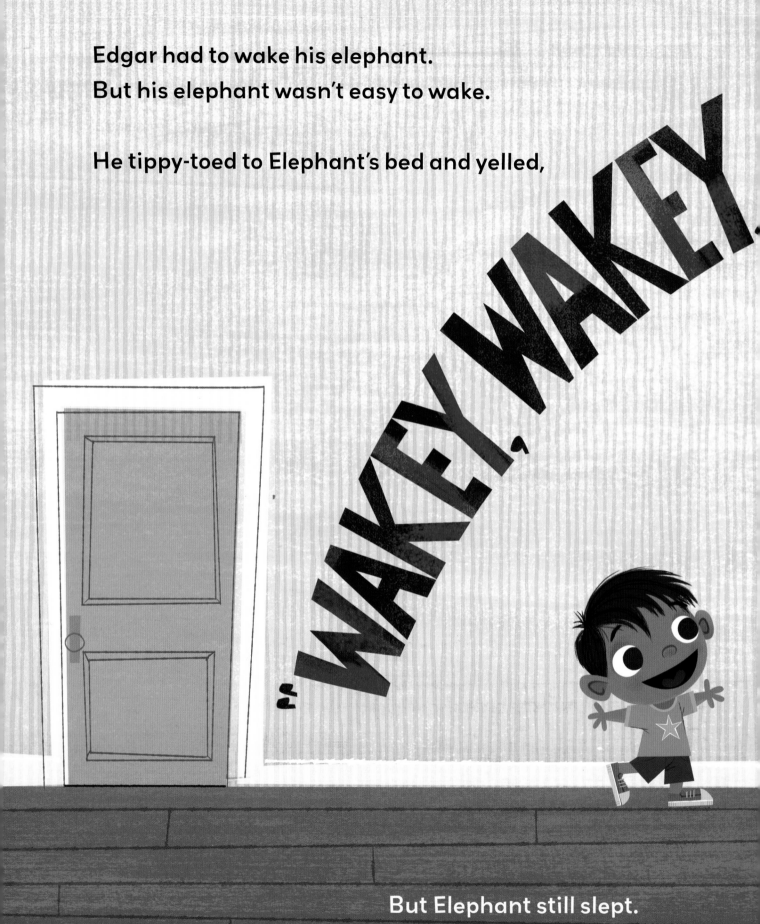

Edgar had to wake his elephant.
But his elephant wasn't easy to wake.

He tippy-toed to Elephant's bed and yelled,

WAKEY, WAKEY.

But Elephant still slept.

He got a feather and tickled him.
Do you think that worked?

No.
Not on *this* elephant.

Edgar then invited a flock of roosters to

COCK-A-DOODLE-DO!

But his friend still slept.

Then Edgar did what anyone who has a sleeping elephant would do. He whipped up a (very noisy) delicious huckleberry banana milkshake, poured every last drop into a too-tall cup with colorful straws, and—

OOPS!

accidently tripped....
But Elephant did not wake up.

Edgar sent over a marching band to parade through Elephant's bedroom.

Rat-a-tat-tat!!!

But Elephant still slept.

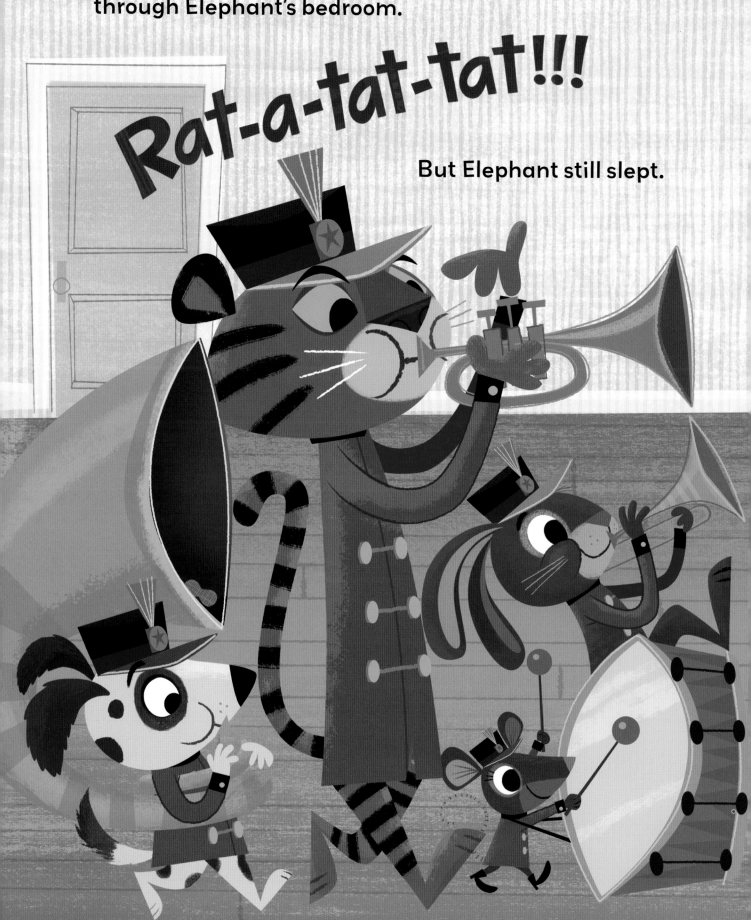

Edgar put a silly hat on Elephant's head.
(The kind with the itchy ruffles.)

And guess
what happened?

Nothing.

So then Edgar did the cha-cha-chicken dance on Elephant's bed.

Made confetti and threw it on him. (The kind that usually made Elephant sneeze.)

Blew up balloons . . .
and POPPED them!

POP!
POP!
POP!
POP!

But Elephant STILL slept.

So then Edgar said, "Shhhhhhhhh . . . let Elephant sleep. He looks so peaceful."

NO, he didn't say that, silly!

Instead he yelled,

"WAKEY,

WAKEY, ELEPHANT!"

And then he . . .

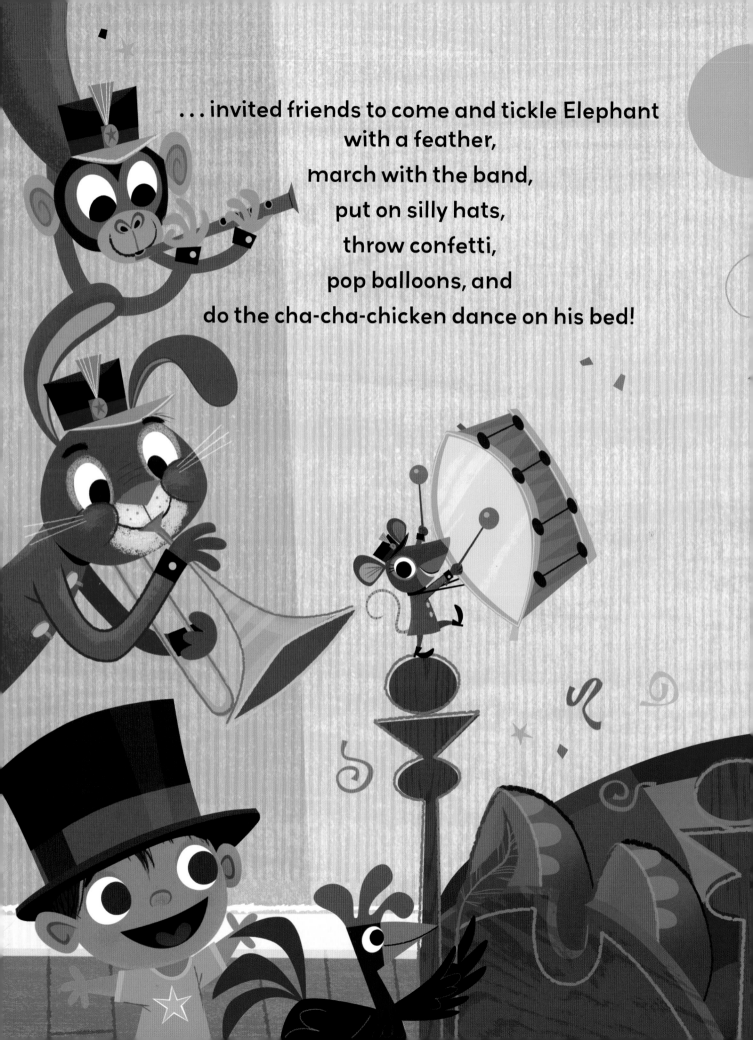

. . . invited friends to come and tickle Elephant
with a feather,
march with the band,
put on silly hats,
throw confetti,
pop balloons, and
do the cha-cha-chicken dance on his bed!

But STILL Elephant slept.

Did Edgar give up?

NO!

He had one more idea.
He stood next to Elephant's bed,
lifted his friend's huge earflap,
and whispered,

"HAPPY ..."
(A little quieter than that.)
"HAPPY BIR ..."
(Even quieter.)
"HAPPY BIRTH ..."

And before Edgar could even finish
. . . can you guess what happened?
(Don't turn the page until you've
taken a guess!)

Elephant leaped out of bed!

He did the cha-cha-chicken dance,

pop-pop-popped balloons,

POP!

threw confetti,
straightened his silly hat,

and marched with the band,
because . . .

. . . today is Elephant's birthday!

Sometimes Elephant forgets things like this and needs a little help remembering.

But the one thing Elephant never forgets is . . .

. . . how lucky he is
to have a friend like Edgar.